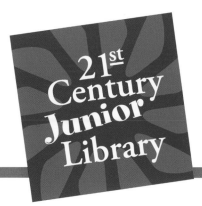

PLANTS
WE EAT

by Christine Petersen

CHERRY LAKE PUBLISHING * ANN ARBOR, MICHIGAN

CHERRY LAKE
Publishing

Published in the United States of America by Cherry Lake Publishing
Ann Arbor, Michigan
www.cherrylakepublishing.com

Content Adviser: Paul Young, MA, Botany

Reading Consultant: Cecilia Minden, PhD, Literacy Specialist and Author

Photo Credits: Cover and page 4, ©Elena Aliaga, used under license from Shutterstock, Inc.; cover and page 6, ©Cornel Achirei, used under license from Shutterstock, Inc.; page 8, ©joanna wnuk, used under license from Shutterstock, Inc.; cover and page 10, ©Steve Smith, used under license from Shutterstock, Inc.; page 12, ©Arco Images GmbH/Alamy; page 14, ©CreativEye99, used under license from Shutterstock, Inc.; page 16, ©Magdalena Zurawska, used under license from Shutterstock, Inc.; page 18, ©iStockphoto.com/ShaneKato; cover and page 20, ©3445128471, used under license from Shutterstock, Inc.

LIBRARY OF CONGRESS CATALOGING-IN-PUBLICATION DATA
Library of Congress Cataloging-in-Publication Data

Petersen, Christine.
 Plants we eat / by Christine Petersen.
    p. cm.—(21st century junior library)
Includes index.
ISBN-13: 978-1-60279-276-0
ISBN-10: 1-60279-276-3
1. Plants, Edible—Study and teaching (Elementary) 2. Crops—Study and
teaching (Elementary) I. Title. II. Series.
QK98.5.A1P48 2008
635—dc22   2008006523

Cherry Lake Publishing would like to acknowledge the work of
The Partnership for 21st Century Skills.
Please visit www.21stcenturyskills.org *for more information.*

CONTENTS

How many of these vegetables can you name?

Where Does Food Come From?

Do you buy most of your food at a market? Did you know that most foods are grown on farms?

Vegetables are plants that people can eat. Some are sent to your local market. You can buy them fresh. Others are used to make foods you buy at grocery stores.

Flour is made from wheat. It is the main ingredient in most breads.

Cereals and bread are made from plants.
Markets sell many foods made from plants.
Let's take a look at the plants people eat.

Make a Guess!

Think about a peanut butter and jelly sandwich. Guess what kinds of plants were used to make the peanut butter. How about the jelly and the bread? Have an adult help you read the labels on those foods. Were your guesses correct?

The green leaves of plants have an important job to do. Many kinds of leaves taste good, too!

Sun Food

Something wonderful happens every day on farms. Plants collect water through their **roots**. Their green leaves take in air and sunlight. Plants use the water, air, and sunlight to make their own food.

Look inside a tomato. You will see the seeds it is protecting.

Sunlight gives plants energy to make food. The food gives the plants energy to grow. They use some food to build longer **stems** and deeper roots. Plants also need energy from food to make flowers. **Fruit** comes from the flowers. Fruits protect seeds. Inside each seed is a tiny new plant.

You can eat many plant parts. They give you energy to live and grow!

Do you like to eat flowers? You do if you like eating cauliflower!

Good Enough to Eat

There are many kinds of **edible** plants in the world! Edible means the plants are safe for people to eat.

Each vegetable has parts that are edible. Carrots are roots. Asparagus is a stem. Potatoes are fat, underground stems called **tubers**. Spinach is a leaf vegetable. Cauliflower is a bunch of flowers you can eat!

Corn is a grain. Each corn kernel has a seed inside.

Fruits have seeds inside. What is your favorite fruit? Is it an apple or a peach? Inside a tomato you will find seeds. A tomato is also a fruit!

Rice and wheat are grains. We eat their seeds. Corn is also a grain. Each corn kernel is a whole fruit with one seed inside. Grains are the most important source of food energy for people all over the world.

When you eat cinnamon, you are eating the bark
from a tree.

Our meals would not be as tasty without **spices**. Cinnamon is made from bark on a tree stem. Pepper is a dried berry. Olive oil comes from the fruit of olive trees.

Here's a surprise. Cookies and candy also have plant items in them. The sugar that makes them sweet comes from plants.

Ask Questions!

Visit your local market. Talk to the person who takes care of the vegetables. Ask how many vegetables the store sells. Find out where the plants are grown. Then try eating a vegetable you have never tasted before!

Carrots are roots. They can be eaten raw or cooked.

The Perfect Meal

Try cooking a meal that contains every plant part. Start with carrots, which are roots. Bell pepper is a fruit. It adds flavor and bright color. Bamboo shoots and bok choy are fun choices for stems. Broccoli is a bunch of flowers. Get fruit and seeds together by tossing in snow peas.

Try to make plants part of every meal you eat!

Ask an adult to help you. Chop up the vegetables. Then heat them in a skillet. What a delicious, healthy meal!

Think!

Write down all the vegetables from your school lunch next week. Put them in groups by color. How many different colors did you eat? Eating many different colors of vegetables will help you stay healthy.

GLOSSARY

edible (ED-uh-buhl) something that is safe to eat

fruit (FROOT) the part of a plant that holds the seeds

roots (ROOTS) underground parts of plants that store plant food

spices (SPYES-ez) something with a strong smell or taste used to flavor food

stems (STEMZ) the long parts of plants from which leaves and flowers grow

tubers (TOO-berz) fat, underground stems that store plant food

vegetables (VEJ-tuh-buhlz) plants grown to be eaten

FIND OUT MORE

BOOKS

Gibbons, Gail. *The Vegetables We Eat*. New York: Holiday House, 2007.

Mayo, Gretchen. *Frozen Vegetables*. Milwaukee, WI: Weekly Reader Early Learning Library, 2004.

WEB SITES

My Dad's Vegetable Garden: The Parts of the Plant We Eat
www.jmu.edu/biology/k12/garden/parts.htm
See more examples of edible plants

MyPyramid.gov— MyPyramid Blast Off Game
www.pyramid.gov/kids/kids_game.html#
Play a game to learn more about vegetables and other healthy food choices

INDEX

ABOUT THE AUTHOR

Christine Petersen is a freelance writer and environmental educator who lives in Minnesota. When she is not writing, Christine enjoys kayaking, bird-watching, and playing with her young son. She is the author of more than 20 books for young people.